Clowns

Written by
Jill Atkins

Clowns are funny.

Clowns make us laugh.

Clowns dress in bright clothes.
They put make-up on their faces.

They paint on a big red mouth
and stick on a round red nose.

This clown has a red jacket.

His pants are odd.
One leg is green and one leg is yellow.

Do you like his wig?

This clown has check pants and striped boots.

His jacket is red, blue, green and yellow.

Do you like the flower on his hat?

This clown has stars on his shirt and hat.

Does he look silly?

This clown has short pants and long boots.

Do you think his hat will fall off?

This clown has six balls.

He can juggle the balls.

Do clowns make you laugh?